For peaceable Peters everywhere.
To Finley, Theo and Wren, with love.
With thanks to Chris. – C.A.

For A.O – S.U.

EGMONT
We bring stories to life

First published in Great Britain 2017 by Egmont UK Limited,
The Yellow Building, 1 Nicholas Road, London W11 4AN
www.egmont.co.uk

Text copyright © Corrinne Averiss 2017
Illustrations copyright © Sam Usher 2017

Corrinne Averiss and Sam Usher have asserted their moral rights.

ISBN 978 1 4052 7819 5

A CIP catalogue record for this title is available from the British Library.

FLOSS
the
PLAYGROUND
BOSS

Corrinne Averiss
Illustrated by Sam Usher

EGMONT

Floss was the playground boss!

Why?

"Because I live next door!"

(But mostly because nobody dared to say otherwise.)

Floss says **stop.**

Floss says **go.**

Floss says **yes.**

Floss says **no!**

Floss says **when.**

Floss says **how.**

Floss says **jump.**

Floss says . . .

now!

Until . . .

. . . a quiet little boy moved into the house on the other side of the playground.

He was called Peter and no one told him that Floss was the boss!

One morning, he launched a paper plane
from the top of the climbing frame.

Whooooosh!

The plane landed right next to Floss's boots.

She was **furious!**

The children stared as Floss ripped Peter's plane into tiny pieces!

"I say stop. I say go.
I say yes.
I say no!
I say over.
I say under.
Hear my great big voice of
THUNDER!"

Everyone waited for Peter to cry.

But he didn't.

He laughed!

Then Peter calmly said,
"I can play wherever I want to!"
and launched another paper plane
into the air!

Whooooosh!

Everyone watched Floss . . . .

as her cheeks

flushed red.

Floss picked up Peter's plane.

"PP2 has been cleared for take-off," said Peter.
"Throw it back to me. Let's play!"

The playground fell silent.

No one
had **ever**
asked Floss
to play before . . .

Floss didn't know what to do.

She looked at the paper plane and wondered

how far she could throw it . . .

But **why** did Peter want to play with **her**?

She was

the Boss!

Who would say stop? Who would say go?

Who would say yes? Who would say no?

Who would say when? Who would say how?

Who would say jump? Who would say now!?

"Clear for take-off!" said Peter again.

"Floss doesn't **play**, she **bosses**!" shouted one brave girl.

"Shhhhhhh!" hissed Floss . . .

... and she hurled the paper plane
into the air with all her might.

It **looped** and **swooped** over everyone's heads until a gust of wind blew it right into Peter's hands!

"Safe landing!" cried Peter.

Floss laughed and clapped before she had time to think about it! The other children had **never** seen Floss having **fun** before!

Peter had pockets **full** of paper planes!

He sent out one after the other as Floss **whizzed** and **zipped** around the playground!

"Ha ha! Come on, everyone! Help me catch them!" she shouted . . . .

. . . and that's just what they did!

Planes flew up.

Planes dived down.

Planes **zoomed** through legs

and **skimmed** noses . . .

... until everyone collapsed in a big giggling pile on the floor!

No one said **stop**. No one said **go**.
No one said **yes**. No one said **no**!
The playground didn't need a boss!

Now Floss the Boss can just be . . .

Floss.

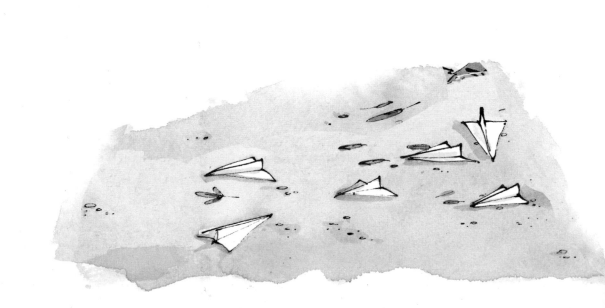